A Plump and Perky Turkey

ISBN 0-439-41798-8

Text copyright © 2001 by Teresa Bateman.
Illustrations copyright © 2001 by Jeff Shelly.
All rights reserved.
Published by Scholastic Inc., 557 Broadway, New York, NY 10012,
by arrangement with Winslow Press. SCHOLASTIC and associated logos
are trademarks and/or registered trademarks of Scholastic Inc.

12 11 10 9 8 7 6 5 4 3 2 1   2 3 4 5 6 7/0

Printed in the U.S.A.   08

First Scholastic printing, November 2002

Creative Director: Bretton Clark
Designed by: Billy Kelly
Editor: Francesca Crispino

The illustrations in this book were prepared with watercolor and gouache.

A Plump and Perky Turkey

To David, Paul, Kirk, Jake, Kris, Sam, and Joey, who would never, ever be fooled by a
clever turkey (even if the turkey were disguised as their aunt!)
T. B.

To my wife, Christine
J. S.

A Plump and Perky Turkey

By Teresa Bateman

Illustrated by Jeff Shelly

SCHOLASTIC INC.
New York Toronto London Auckland Sydney
Mexico City New Delhi Hong Kong Buenos Aires

The people in Squawk Valley
were downhearted and depressed.
Thanksgiving was approaching,
but without its special guest.
They couldn't find a turkey
for the feast they planned to eat.
It looked like they'd be making do
with bowls of shredded wheat.

"A plump and perky turkey's
    what we need," they all agreed.
"But finding turkeys nowadays
    is very hard indeed.
The birds have gotten smarter,
    and they all seem quite aware
that it's best to disappear
    when autumn leaves are in the air."
A plump and perky turkey—
    stomachs rumbled at the thought.
But how to trick a turkey
    into jumping in the pot?

Then Ebenezer Beezer
	had a thought pop in his head.
"If we can't find a turkey,
	let's have one find us, instead!
We could hold an arts-and-crafts fair,"
	he declared, with wink and grin.
"A fair with one grand turkey prize—
	that *all* of us could win!

And since our goal is turkey,
    that's the theme we'll take to heart.
We'll fill our fair with folks and fun
    and tons of turkey art.

We'll make turkeys out of spuds

and out of clay and out of rope.

We'll make turkeys out of oatmeal,

out of paper, out of soap!

We'll hang a bunch of posters
in the forest way down low,
to invite some turkey candidates
to model for our show.
Why, even turkeys understand
(as everybody knows)
you can't make turkey art
without a turkey there to pose."

The people in Squawk Valley
held a poster jamboree!
They plastered their creations
onto every single tree.

Now it happened in Squawk Valley,
   lived a turkey known as Pete.
He was cocky, he was clever,
   and he really liked to eat.
While he strutted through the forest,
   plump and perky through the pines,
he was startled, and intrigued,
   by all those interesting signs.
With a proud and jaunty gobble,
   he gave out a hearty cry—
"A plump and perky turkey?
   Well, I'm sure I qualify."

Pete applied for the position,
 and he strutted plump and proud.
He could hardly wait to model
 for the large and eager crowd.
"Yer hired!" shouted Beezer,
 for the folks had all agreed
that Pete the Perky Turkey
 was the answer to their need.

'Twas the week before Thanksgiving
when Pete posed to do his part,
and the artsy-craftsy townsfolk
started making turkey art.

They made turkeys out of spuds

and out of clay and out of rope.

They made turkeys out of oatmeal,

out of paper, out of soap.

Thanksgiving Day, the artwork done,
    they asked the model down,
to judge their homemade turkeys
    and to pick the best in town.
"Now when the judging's over,"
    Beezer whispered with a smile,
"we'll tuck that model turkey
    in the oven for a while."

Pete judged each piece of artwork
as the hungry crowd all cheered.
He stopped to take a closer look,
and then . . . he disappeared!

There were turkeys made of spuds,
    there were turkeys made of rope.
There were turkeys made of paper,
    there were turkeys made of soap.
The room was full of turkeys,
    in a wall-to-wall collage.
For a clever bird like Pete
    it was a perfect camouflage.

"He's over here!" Old Beezer said.

"He's here!" said Jacob Green.

They searched amongst the turkeys,
but their bird had fled the scene.

A note in turkey scrawl they found,
half-hidden on the lawn:
"Good-bye. I took my modeling fee."
(The oatmeal bird was gone.)

The people in Squawk Valley
were left feeling rather blue.
The only turkeys left in town
appeared too hard to chew.
"Oh well," said Beezer brightly,
as they gathered 'round to eat.
"Right now, at least I'm thankful
that we still have shredded wheat."

That day folks learned a lesson
that stuck firm with them forever.
A plump and perky turkey
can be pretty doggone clever.